HE SAID FOREVER... HE LIED!

Deception: He Lied Miniseries

Daphne Dennis

TLM Publishing House

Copyright

Copyright © 2022 Daphne Dennis, TLM Publishing House

Social Stamina – 1,2,3 Let's Go!

Titles to help look at things from other perspectives and strengthen your mindset.

The Great Ascension–1,2,3 Let's Go!

Titles to help you gain focus and climb the ladder of success!

How to Start – 1,2,3 Let's Go!

Titles to help you with step-by-step, must-have knowledge of the business world and personal experiences.

Top 10 Questions to Ask Before You…1,2,3 Let's Go!

Titles with must-have questions (and logic behind) for many of life's daily and major decisions.

Find our fiction below!

https://www.ttpublishinghouse.com/legendsreborn

https://www.ttpublishinghouse.com/7wishes

https://www.ttpublishinghouse.com/mallcadet

Social Media

Facebook: tlmpublishinghouse

Website: www.TTpublishinghouse.com

Want to Read for Free?

You may qualify for a spot on our Advance Reader Copy group.

Never heard of an ARC Group?

Simply put, it's a small group of people who are interested in a specific genre and are invited to read books before they're published.

Your feedback can help alter the storyline or even catch an elusive typo!

You're asked to provide an honest review when it is published, and that's it!

You read for free!

Go now to confirm your interest in the ARC Group!
https://www.ttpublishinghouse.com/joinTLMarc

Contents

Transactions

Fuck. Fuck. Fuck. Fuck.

Debbie stood in front of the square, one-story stucco building, shaking like a presidential candidate about to give a speech. It was time to make a change. *I can't go on the way I have been. I have to know the truth. Why am I so frightened to do what needs to be done?* Debbie thought as she approached the ATM.

Her first order of business was to check her account balance. She assumed the square ATM machine was surrounded by blue to make people feel calm and invited, but she did not feel calm, nor invited. Last week, $5,000 had gone missing from her joint bank account. Well, technically, it didn't go missing. The bank statement showed that there had been a withdrawal, but only she or her husband, Ed, were allowed to withdraw from that account. Clearly, It didn't inexplicably disappear. However, when she asked Ed about it, he said he hadn't withdrawn anything, and it must be a bank error.

"Really, Ed? A $5,000 bank error? We need to go down there to the bank and get this straightened out!" Debbie adamantly put her foot down. For some reason, Ed didn't seem to be concerned about it though. Usually, if any bank or credit card statement was even a dollar off, he'd usually be tracking it down like a bloodhound on a fresh scent. Nope, this wasn't like him at all.

Ed and Debbie have lived in this geographically diverse, suburban section of the world pretty much all her life. She lived in an area that held some of the world's oldest and tallest trees, great little isolated beaches, and the rockiest terrain perfect for nature hikes. Anyone on the outside of Debbie's life, looking in, would say she has a perfect life. In fact, Debbie went through nearly twenty years on auto-pilot of perfection.

Sure, she had her ups and downs, like the time she started to put on weight and felt she was losing her youthful beauty; but she had never been through a crisis like this before. Her life had been moving along like a river, but she had no control over how the water flowed.

I have to take control of my life. I can't keep being someone elses' supporting character anymore! I've literally lived my life for others, and how do they thank me? By secretly taking out our savings? Maybe she was blowing it all out of proportion like Ed had told her.

"Now settle down, honey, I'm sure the bank will figure it out and get it corrected any day now. You just let me handle this. Can you grab me a bottle of mineral water?" Ed asked her, hoping to change the subject.

Yeah, Debbie knew that some would call her life ideal, but she felt like it was unraveling, and everything she cared about was slipping away from her.

"God, please let the money be back." Debbie sent up a prayer just in case she had any pull with the Big Guy. She had stopped by the ATM on the way home from getting some groceries, that she didn't even need, just to give herself an excuse to go out without being suspicious. She felt awful for even considering Ed might be up to no good. He hadn't given her a reason to suspect anything crazy before. Sure, he'd never be on the cover of Good Housekeeping or Family Man, but he'd always taken good care of her.

Four, four, three, seven.

Invalid pin code. Please re-enter.

Four. Four. Three. Seven. Oh shit, did I do four, four, *three*, seven or four, *three*, three, seven? Ugh... "Four. Four. Three-

Fucking-Seven" Debbie said, as she dramatically pushed each key. *Pull it together dumbass. You're lucky no one heard your pin code. Geez, what if I said the pin code before and someone somehow used it? Stop! Stop! You didn't do this!*

She pressed the lifeless keys of the machine and examined the balance. "What the Actual Fuck?" Not only was the $5,000 *not* back in their account, but there was also money missing. *Oh, my God.* She thought as she looked at the numbers. She felt sick. Another $10,000 had been taken out. Debbie rubbed her forehead frantically. *What is happening? Is someone stealing it? This can't be a mistake. Two major withdrawals, and somehow Ed, hasn't freaked out about it?*

She stood there in disbelief as her hair blew in the breeze. Debbie knew that the most likely reason the money was missing was that Ed was taking it out. They were the only two who could access the account. There was no other explanation that made any sense. *Why would Ed take money like this and not tell me about it?*

Why had he withdrawn so much cash from the account? He had always been a somewhat mysterious man. He was a nuclear physicist, and she was pretty sure he made bombs for a living, maybe diffused them, or perhaps made lasers that could shoot them down. She wasn't sure of the details. He was legally not allowed to talk about it.

But, since he had retired, he had become more secretive than ever. She'd noticed that he always looked so good nowadays. In the past, he had never put in that much effort regarding his appearance. Ed usually wore a beard to complement his round face, which was increasingly gray. He liked to keep his hair a little bit longer. Last month, he'd gone out and gotten a $50 haircut, the type he used to make fun of, plus he usually wore a flannel over his work clothes. But, lately, he had been shaving and dressing in suits (minus the flannel). *Why is Ed acting so differently nowadays? There is definitely something going on here. I wonder if he is seeing another woman.*

Debbie opened her purse and pulled out 5 checks. *Should I even cash these? Or will this money get taken out too?* She heard a noise behind her and turned around. She saw a lady standing behind her, a well-dressed woman with olive skin and black hair.

"Is this going to take much longer?" The woman asked.

"No," Debbie replied.

She pushed the checks back into her purse and returned to her red sedan. She got in and put the car in drive, taking her whirlwind of emotions out on the steering wheel. *Things have to be different now. I can't live like this anymore.* Debbie thought of the scenarios that would have been okay for Ed to have taken out the money without telling her. A gift? A vacation? Nah, that wasn't Ed's MO, and he'd never take that kind of money out without talking about it.

While driving home, she began to think about everything that was happening. There were several signs that something was going on with Ed. His appearance and he had become so elusive. He'd shut off his computer when she'd walk into the bedroom. He always hid his phone from her as if guarding some terrible secret. There were instances when she'd tried to call him, and his phone went straight to voicemail. Even when he was still working, he'd never give her 'the button.' Plus, he never touched her anymore or seemed to want to be with her. *He doesn't seem to care about me anymore. He doesn't notice me at all.* Debbie snapped her focus back to her driving and realized she'd already made it to her driveway. Well, I guess it's time for a showdown!

***

Debbie rushed straight into the house, leaving the groceries behind in the car. She had mustered up the courage for the confrontation. It was time. She was sure that by now, Ed had prepared his breakfast and would likely be at the breakfast bar. She used to make him breakfast every morning. But now that she was working, and he wasn't, she had started buying ready-made bacon and pancakes. *I cooked for him all that time, and he never even thanked me. I should have started making him cook his own breakfast years ago, she fumed to herself as she turned the corner into the dining area.*

She found Ed sitting at the head of the dining table—not entirely weird to see him there, but Debbie thought it a bit odd since he usually would just eat at the counter to avoid dirtying up the table. She sat down, across from Ed, afraid to sit beside him, in case things escalated. No, she wasn't afraid of him or his reaction, but of her own. She didn't want to accuse him of anything until she was certain what was going on, but it was time to push for an answer. She rubbed the back of her neck. *Why am I doing this? How did it come to this?*

Ed sat, reading his paper, his breakfast plate pushed aside. Ed was a tall man of medium weight, with dark brown hair, with more and more gray strands appearing. He was of Scottish and Irish descent. He often boasted that he was most likely related to William Wallace. Debbie doubted that.

"How was the breakfast?" she inquired, trying to get him engaged in some small talk before letting him have it, as she made short jerky movements with her hands. She always talked with her hands. But, today, her hands weren't making any sense.

"It's ridiculous," she heard him say.

She stood up, flaring her nostrils, "Well, *you're* ridiculous!"

"No, I said, it's delicious." He stared at her blankly and then looked back at his paper.

Debbie sat back down. Her cheeks turned red, embarrassed to have misunderstood his words at such a vital moment. "I need to talk to you about something. Please put down your paper."

"Go ahead, talk to me. We can talk while I read the newspaper." He responded. He sighed heavily and narrowed his eyes.

"No, we can't talk when you're reading the paper." Ed put down the paper, clenching his jaw as though it was the worst thing ever happening to him. Come on, this is serious.

Debbie leaned in closer to Ed. "We must have an important discussion about something." She stated. "A serious talk is necessary. I'm curious as to why you leave every day. I have no clue where you are going. Seriously, where do you go when you leave the house in the morning?"

"Out." He replied in a sharp tone.

"So, you drive around? Do you have a destination, or do you just drive to around for hours, using up gas just to avoid being at home?" She asked in an even, serious tone.

"No," Ed replied while squirming in his chair.

"That was actually not a yes or no question. It drives me crazy that for 25 years you were a workaholic, and now that you're retired, you're still never home. At least back then, you were home on the weekends even though we never spent time together. Either you were upstairs in the bedroom, glued to your computer, or you had friends over playing some world domination game. I mean, why couldn't you have at least played something that I could have played too? You know I don't like those silly war games. I like word games. You know that, but getting you to play something I'd enjoy was like asking you to shave your legs or something. I know that global conquest is your pastime, but I've been unhappy because I felt like I was in a war of my own, but mine was against your job, your friends, and now, who knows what the hell I'm fighting against for your attention!"

Debbie continued talking, feeling like she was babbling. "Maybe I'm too nice. That's my problem. But then again, nothing would have gotten done if I hadn't been. What I'm trying to say, Ed, is that there's another ten thousand dollars missing from the account. I just checked, in hopes that the other five thousand would be back, but it's not back Ed. Do you know anything about that?" She asked as she tried to keep a calm exterior.

"No," Ed replied, as he avoided eye contact with her. She knew he was lying. For him to be so calm at her telling him that there is now fifteen thousand dollars missing, she knew it in her toes, he'd taken the money out. But why? What's the big mystery?

"Come on, Ed, it doesn't make any sense. Two plus two equals 4, not 0. My math skills may not be great, but I know enough math to know that. Stop lying to me. I get that you think I'm dumb, but do you really think I'm this fucking stupid?" She got up and started pacing in a manic way. "Is there another woman?" She asked.

"No."

"Come on, this is ridiculous!" She clenched her hands into fists. "Who else could have taken it? It's a joint account. It sure as hell wasn't me! And why are you shaving lately? It's OK, Ed, I won't get upset. Just tell me the truth. Tell me why you took it." Her eyes bulged, and she looked at him with a pained stare.

"No." He said defensively.

Debbie continued to pace around the kitchen, clinching and unclinching her hands. She pointed at the door. She turned to him, looked him square in the eye, planted her feet wide apart, and shouted, "Then, get out!"

Ed looked toward Debbie, gauging her expression. Debbie recognized his questioning gaze and knew she had to remain resolute. *Don't you dare weaken now, he's finally taking you seriously,* she thought to herself.

"I know it might seem shocking that I am kicking you out. You like to think that you control everything because I've let you all these years. I let you because I believed you were a good and trustworthy man who had my best interest at heart. I let you because we agreed that you'd pay the bills and I'd take care of the house and the kids... and you Ed. And I did. I took great care of everyone and everything, and all I asked for was to know that we were in this together. We were a team...and we trusted each other!

But if we can't trust each other, I made this house a home, and I refuse to leave it unless you give me no choice. I'm the one who decorated it and designed the interior. I'm the one who cleans it and takes care of it. And I can't live here with someone who is lying to me. So, tell me, or leave." She choked as her eyes well up.

"OK. I'll go," he answered as the color drained from his face.

***

Debbie wished that Ed had chosen the other option. Ed went upstairs to pack, and Debbie began questioning whether she had made the correct decision to confront him. She was having second thoughts about kicking him out. She sat down at the dining room table, staring at the floor. Her thoughts began to move quickly and erratically, but she couldn't move.

Why did I kick him out? Is that really what I should have done? What's going to happen to me now?

It took him barely thirty minutes to pack the bulk of his belongings. He was a simple man, particularly now that he had a kindle reader and all his books were on his tablet. Almost everything he had was contained in his laptop bag, a suitcase, and a camping duffle bag for his clothing and toiletries. His clothes barely filled half of his closet, and those he did have tended to look precisely the same. He did not like variety.

As Ed descended from upstairs, he saw Debbie and lowered his gaze. He walked to the door with his bags in hand, opened it, and went out. Debbie followed him silently. Ed turned around and looked at her and said, "Bye."

It was agonizing for Debbie. She dabbed a tissue at her wet, dull eyes. She wished she didn't feel so miserable about it, but she did. A tear streamed down her face. She wanted to tell him to come back inside and just talk to her. She tried to say she was sorry for her mistake, but no words would come out.

No, this can't be happening. What did I do? Is this really the end? She was unable to speak. And the next thing she knew, he was in his little white hatchback car, and, in another minute, he was gone.

***

Grief

Debbie went back into the house. She was alone now. She didn't have to pretend not to care or fake being stronger than she really felt. She was free to ugly-cry now. She collapsed onto the couch and smashed her face into a couch pillow and screamed until she lost the strength to continue. Fluffy, her dog, sat at the couch, afraid to jump up. Clearly even Fluffy knew that something very different was happening.

"Hey boy. How ya' doin'? You still love me, don't ya?" She asked as she scooped Fluffy up from the floor and cuddled into him; hoping at least with his presence, she wouldn't feel so alone. He didn't respond.

"Oh, how am I?" She pretended to have a conversation with him. "Not so good." Fluffy was the only one who understood her.

"We'll have to discuss it later. I have to get ready for work." That morning, getting ready for work was miserable. She walked upstairs to her bedroom and got dressed in one of her exquisite pantsuits, which, by the way, Ed had never said anything about.

She looked fantastic. *I look amazing in these pants suits. Why did Ed never notice? I'm not bad looking for a woman in her 50s. Why doesn't he appreciate anything?* She applied her makeup and then started to cry again. *Will this day ever end?*

She went out of the house and into her red sedan. The route to work was rather picturesque since she had to drive on windy roads up and down the hills to get to her job. It was a long journey to the vineyard and honestly, it was usually a great opportunity for Debbie to have some windshield time to keep her thoughts together. Today though, Debbie's thoughts were anything but together.

There were many trees and vineyards, and it was charming when the sun rose, but this morning it did not feel lovely to her. Her eyelids felt hot and gummy from crying. She had a sensation of utter and absolute bitterness. It was so aggravating that she lived in such a wonderful area, a suburban paradise, but everything seemed so chaotic. She wished she could enjoy all the beauty, but she couldn't. *Why couldn't Ed have gone out with me more?*

She continued driving while attempting to sort things out. Had she made the correct decision? She was beginning to regret the decision once again but trying to hold it together. She had to erase the memory from her mind. What else could she possibly think about? She didn't want to crash. As she followed the road to the top of the hill, she could see the ocean close by, despite her efforts to avoid looking at it. There, the water was so lovely. The waves smashed into the sand with splendor. *This is so beautiful. I should have gone to see the sunrise every morning. I can't believe how much I've missed.*

Because of the sunrise, the sky was filled with vibrant hues like orange, yellow, and pink. *I am so foolish. What have I done with my life?*

After descending the hill, she passed by various paths where bike races had taken place. She drove by a farmer's market. She'd always planned to visit the farmers' market but never did. Why hadn't she found the time? *What have I even done with life? I wasted so many years caring for a man who didn't care about me.* Why hadn't she made the most of these opportunities? She had never attended the annual New Year's celebration or any of the fireworks shows. Why hadn't she gone? Because Ed didn't like those sorts of things. She could have gone alone but she chose to stay by Ed's side no matter how much she wanted to go. She wished she could turn back time and be young again.

She had scheduled unforgettable get-togethers with her friends, family members, and coworkers. Still, She hadn't done so many of the things that interested her. She blamed Ed. He was different from she was. He was an intellectual, or, so he said, whatever that meant. He certainly had accomplished a great deal. He was a nuclear physicist, but she was beginning to question if she had ever known who he really was. She wished she had realized earlier what his character was really like.

She had spent her life planning parties, cooking for people, and bringing them snacks. She listened intently to guests and tried to entertain them with her stories. *What was the point of all of it?*

Arriving at the vineyard, Debbie was always proud to work with this winery. It offered a stunning space to sip the world's best wine. This winery is well-renowned in the city. It introduced a choice of expertly crafted food and wine experiences in addition to a revamped appearance that mixed contemporary features with classic aspects. Outside was an open grassy area with a beautiful backdrop for lawn sports and al fresco wine service. She saw her friend Pattie as she entered.

"Hello, Patti. How are you doing?" Debbie asked.

"I'm OK, sweetie. How are you, darling?" Her friend replied.

Usually, she liked seeing her friend, but at that moment, she wanted to run away. "My life is awful. Ed left."

***

Debbie's employer, Al, walked up to her. She usually enjoyed talking with people, but she wished he had just passed by that morning.

"I'm going to go into the cellar and organize the new wine stock," she said to him.

"Why do you want to do that?" He inquired. "That isn't one of your responsibilities." Debbie had a guilty look on her face. She just wanted to go somewhere and spend some time alone, which wasn't typical of her. *How am I going to make it through this day?*

"I'm just in the mood to get things organized." She felt awkward, having trouble thinking what to say, which wasn't like her.

"I'll go with you," Patty chirped. Her medium brown, shoulder-length hair was slightly curled at the bottom.

"It's no problem," Debbie said. She still felt terrible, as if she had done something wrong.

"I'll help you," Patty expressed in an optimistic tone. Debbie usually liked Patty's optimism, but that morning it annoyed her.

"OK," Debbie replied. *I just want to be alone right now. Why is it so shocking?* She couldn't argue with Patty. They walked together to the wine cellar, where a bunch of new boxes had arrived. It was an underground wine cellar. This winery used ground temperature to decrease temperature fluctuations and make them seasonal rather than daily.

Debbie began opening boxes and putting bottles away.

"Ed left you, huh?" Patty inquired, full of intrigue. "Oh, no! You must be heartbroken. When Charles and I split up, it was the same way. Men, especially those smart ones, can't be trusted. Some folks have all brains and no heart. It will take some time for you to recover. You'll have to go through all of the stages of grief. I'll try to remember what they are so I can tell you about them."

Debbie's features tightened. *I just want to be alone.* She did not like discussing Ed. *I'm not sure how I will get her to talk about anything else. I'd rather talk about something else, anything else.*

"No, Patty, it's alright," Debbie said. "You don't have to talk about the phases of grief. I'm not grieving. I'm wonderful. I'd like to think about anything else right now," Patty said.

"Denial," Patty said, delighted that she had recalled it. *The first stage of grief is denial?*

Debbie kept on opening more boxes. She had no idea she was grieving. Debbie's nostrils were flaring. "Right now, I don't want to deal with it. Patty. I just need some time." *Was I living in denial? Am I really going through the grieving process?*

"That's exactly right," Patty said. Debbie pursed her lips together. "That is exactly what you should do. Take as much time as you need to think. It took ten years for me to get over Charles."

Patty continued to babble. *This isn't helping.* "To be honest, it'll likely take you much longer than that. Because you and Ed have been married for a longer period than we were." She went on.

"Patty, we're *still* married," Debbie replied, raising her voice.

"I understand, but I feel compelled to tell you that I saw the writing on the wall. Ed is a jerk." In most cases, Debbie would have defended Ed, claiming that Patty was misinterpreting his behavior, saying that he was an introvert.

She wasn't sure whether she believed that or not anymore. She didn't feel like defending him. Talking about Ed made her feel like she was going to get an ulcer. *How can I get Patty to talk about something else?*

"I'm afraid I won't be able to say anything about it. Soon, I'll have to start the tour." Debbie needed to get into her tour mindset. She had a group of people coming over, but she was not in the mood to give the tour. *How am I going to smile and pretend like everything is OK? I just had my heart ripped out.*

"Debbie, you know how much I love you, right?"

"Yes, I know that you do. And I appreciate your friendship. I'm not sure what I'd do without you. But just please promise me that you won't tell anyone. And don't talk about it anymore! I don't want anyone to know *it's a private matter."*

"I won't tell anyone. Your secret is safe with me."

"There's my miracle saleswoman and her helper. How is everything going?" In front of her stood her boss, Al. He had a scruffy face, dark-rimmed glasses, and a blue shirt with white dots.

"Her husband left her," Patty said.

"Oh," Al rubbed the back of his neck. "Oh, that's…." He escaped the room.

"You shouldn't have said anything to him, Patty. He's our boss. And also, he's a man. Men have no idea what to say or do regarding feelings. You embarrassed him." Debbie said to Patty, moving her arms around with sweeping gestures. *Actually, you embarrassed me. What am I going to do with you, Patty?*

"Sorry, I was just trying to help you. I didn't think you meant him when you said not to tell anyone." She defended herself, pouting like a small child.

"OK, it's alright, but please don't tell anyone else about the situation," Debbie said. She felt bad for scolding her friend.

"OK, I won't. I'm not going to say anything. I promise."

***

The Unwelcome Guest

Debbie gazed at the vineyard. The grape vines were planted in rows. To keep them off the ground, wooden structures supported them, and the white-fleshed fruit grew in clusters with purple skins. Debbie usually led various tours multiple times a day, explaining the winery's history back to the 1800s. As she gazed at the vineyard, she thought of Ed. They had gone on so many strolls in that place, holding hands.

The caves, introducing them to the winemakers and conducting the wine tasting portion of the tour. The tour group arrived, and Debbie led the tour, showing them the vineyard. She was supposed to be informing them of the vineyard's history and operations. Still, she kept interjecting sad comments, like, "This is a nice place for lovers to stroll, although it's sad after they break up."

The guests sat outside on the winery's porch on wood tables. Cheese and wine tasting was the final portion of the tour and usually everyone's favorite. That was usually her favorite part too. But she wasn't in the mood that day. It seemed as if everything she said fell flat and was monotoned.

Debbie overheard Patty tell one of the visitors, "She's usually more entertaining. Her husband left her." *Patty, what are you doing?*

Just then, Debbie's mom showed up wearing black slacks with black high heel boots and a leopard-printed jacket. "Deborah," her mother said.

"What are you doing here, Mother? I'm in the middle of a tour." Debbie said with feigned concern.

"That is a lovely way to greet your mother. It's also great to see you." Debbie's mother remarked sarcastically as she raised her chin.

"I didn't mean to be rude, mom. It's great to see you too. I just don't have time to talk to you right now." Debbie drew herself up to her full height.

"This is an emergency, Deborah. I need to speak with you ASAP." Debbie's mom said, flaring her nostrils.

"What could be so urgent that you can't wait another five minutes for the tour to finish?" Debbie crossed her arms as she asked.

"I can take over," Patty suggested. "It's all right. You should talk to your mom."

"Thank you very much," Debbie forced a smile to Patty as Debbie and her mother entered the winery structure. The foyer of the building had beautiful wood floors made of authentic natural wood, tall tables lining the front wall, with equally tall stools to match. Above the table, large glass windows were reaching the ceiling that let in the natural sunlight. Debbie's mom led her to one of the tables and sat down. Debbie followed her lead and sat down across from her.

"OK, mom, what exactly do you want to discuss with me?" Debbie asked, gazing at her in a challenging way, full of judgment.

"I heard your husband left." Debbie's mom said as she glared at her.

"Have you already heard that? It happened this morning." Debbie pushed her shoulders back and her chest out, bracing for a fight.

Patty. "News travels quickly, as we all know. Patty texted me," she said, showing Debbie her phone.

"Ed leaving isn't something I want to discuss. It isn't your problem. Don't worry about it. I've got it all figured out." Debbie stared at her mom, refusing to be the one to break eye contact.

"You've got it all figured out, do you? I don't believe that. I'm relieved, Deborah. He never was my favorite person. He's a horrid man who never appreciated you." She wrinkled her nose.

"I know that you never liked him. But I did. It was my choice. *Mine.*" Debbie tossed her head.

"No, I didn't like him because he would go upstairs and avoid everyone whenever you hosted a party at your place." *I would have gone upstairs to get away from you too, Debbie held herself back from replying.* Debbie normally would have defended him by claiming he was an introvert, but she did not want to do that now.

"Now that you're aware, I'd best go back to work." Debbie got up to leave.

"I didn't come here to say that. Deborah, you need to get your act together. You're a gifted woman who might have accomplished great things with your life. However, you decided to waste it with Ed. And now you're squandering it in this pitiful job." She stroked her throat and grimaced.

"What exactly do you mean by pitiful? I'm fantastic at what I do." Debbie put her hands on her hips.

"Yes, that's why I stated that you're gifted, but you're wasting your abilities by working for someone else. As I always tell you, you should start your own business." She shook her head.

"I get what you're saying. But I don't know how to do that."

"You have no idea because you have never tried." Debbie's mom replied, shuttering.

"It's not like I can simply go out and purchase a winery. These places, after all, are handed down from generation to generation. They are hardly ever sold by the families that own them." Debbie inhaled deeply. *I've had enough of this. I'm walking away.*

"OK, Deborah, let's change the topic." Debbie gritted her teeth. *Why does mom always win?* "I came to let you know that I'm organizing a get-together. An old friend of mine has his son in town this week, and I want you to meet him. He's a very successful and wealthy man."

"What exactly do you mean? Ed and I have been separated for a few hours, and you want me to meet someone else?" Debbie subconsciously put her hands into fists.

"Well, you know, Deborah, if you had just listened to me and followed my advice in the first place, you would have been able to meet a suitable person right away and wouldn't have wasted 25 years of your life." She raised her voice, shaking her head.

"I squandered 25 years of my life?" Deborah raised her voice, flaring her nostrils.

"If you're going to speak to me in this tone, I'm sorry, but I must leave. Really, I only came here to be of help. Goodbye." Debbie's mom got out of her seat and walked away. *How does she always win?*

***

As Debbie walked into her home that night, she thought, *I squandered 25 years of my life.* Debbie wanted to watch some television. Her living room's warm, inviting aura made her want to snuggle up, rest, and withdraw from the world. She grabbed fluffy pillows and a soft throw and cuddled up near the warmly illuminated artificial fireplace and grabbed the remote control.

After all, it had been a long time since she'd completely controlled the remote. She was even looking forward to watching some of her favorite programs, notably her favorite murder mystery series, Crime Investigation. She flipped to the channel where she knew it would be on. *Everyone tries to control me. Finally, I can do what I want, with no one telling me what to do. First my mom, then Ed. But, no more.*

She grabbed a bottle of wine from the wine fridge and grabbed a glass and corkscrew. Opening a new bottle of wine always felt like a special occasion for some reason. She hoped it would help her bust out of these blues, but so far, it hadn't. Debbie poured herself a glass of wine and drank it quickly, with purpose. She had to unwind. It was beautiful to just have to cook for one person. She was free to eat anything she pleased. *If this is so wonderful, then why do I feel so sad? Why do I still have feelings for Ed when I'm so angry with him?*

Her phone beeped as she watched her show, so she glanced down at it. There were new missing people notifications. *They're probably just people who have dementia and have wandered away.* Fluffy rushed up to her and hopped onto her arm on the sofa.

"You're the only one who understands me, Fluffy." Fluffy was a Maltipoo, a hybrid between a Maltese and a miniature poodle. Cuteness, loyalty, and intellect were the attributes that made this breed renowned. That was why Debbie had gotten him.

"I should have told you about my problems instead of Patty." Fluffy barked. "Yes, you understand. I'm sure you understand what I'm talking about."

Having a little peace and quiet was quite calming, and Debbie was a big fan of wine. *I'm on my own now. I'm so lucky.* She was raised in wine country, after all. She needed to do something to take her mind off Ed. She grabbed her notebook from her end table. She started planning how she would fix up her garden and drawing her new landscaping ideas.

It was good that she had her own work and was now earning her own money, money that she could spend however she pleased without asking for Ed's approval. *I'm an independent woman now. No one will tell me what to do. No one.* A tear fell on her cheek. Ironically, Ed seemed to have spent a significant amount of their money without asking or informing her about it.

This was her time to shine, to redefine herself. It was now or never, time for her to display her true colors. *I can conquer the world if I set my mind to it.*

She began checking her phone for messages. She recalled receiving a text from an old friend, Judy, a month earlier. It was an invitation to come to visit her in her cabin in the mountains.

Debbie had forgotten about it. Honestly, at the time, it seemed a little strange. Judy wasn't a close friend. She was only a casual acquaintance. Even so, Judy was good about staying in touch. She had phoned Debbie once a month to check up on her. Then, out of nowhere, she asked her to stay with her. Given their level of friendship, it felt a little too intimate, so she opted to just ignore the message at the time.

I completely forgot to respond to that SMS. I should've responded to her. How rude of me. Debbie decided to text Judy. Even better, she would call her. The phone began to ring as Debbie pressed the contact number, but no one answered. The phone didn't even ring. It was immediately routed to voicemail. Debbie left a message, "Hello, Judy. I apologize for the delay in responding, but I'd love to see you at your cabin. Yes, that seems to be a fantastic idea. Please call me back as soon as possible."

Debbie's thoughts continued to race despite her efforts to calm herself down. She could think of nothing but Ed. *Why did he leave me? I know I told him to go, but wouldn't any normal woman expect her man to fight to stay together? Why doesn't he love me anymore?* By now, tears were streaming down her face freely. She finished the second bottle of wine and fell asleep on the couch in her clothes with the TV on.

***

Are You Home?

In the morning, when Debbie woke up, she realized that her makeup was smeared all over her face. Then it dawned on her what she had done. She looked at her phone to check the time. *No, no, no. I overslept.* She dashed upstairs, getting ready quickly. She looked in her closet and saw her navy-blue pants suit and threw it on. No time for makeup today!

When she got to work, Patty wanted to talk about nothing except how bad men are, particularly snooty men who are brilliant. Debbie went to the cellar again to unload more boxes of wine. Patty followed her. "You know you don't have to do this, right? This is my job."

"I know. But I need to do something. I can't be idle. When I'm not doing anything, I start thinking about Ed. I'm just so angry with him." Debbie said as her eyebrows furrowed.

"That's the second stage of grief. You're going through the phases quickly. I see your point about Ed. You know, after all these years, I finally figured out that you should always be with a man who isn't as smart as you are," she said to Debbie. "That way, he won't be able to deceive you. Find a simple man. That is my new way of thinking." Patty said with a sour expression on her face.

"So, you've decided you don't like intelligent people anymore?"

"No, I don't think so. Certain types of intelligence are OK, like social intelligence and emotional intelligence. Those are valuable assets. When it comes to math and science, however, intelligence is a left-brain phenomenon. People with those gifts can't be trusted. That was Charles' personality."

"I'm beginning to reach the same conclusion as you. I'm not a fan of smart people either anymore. Scientists in particular. Bomb makers and nuclear physicists are the worst. They definitely can't be trusted." Debbie said as her chin trembled. "Now, can we talk about something else?"

Debbie and Patty finished unpacking the wine boxes early. Now there was nothing to do. "Let's go out front and find something to do," Debbie said.

Once they entered the front of the vineyard, Debbie noticed a woman entering. Debbie knew the woman. She was a notorious gossip, but, at the same time, she had money and liked wine. Debbie figured this was an excellent opportunity to make a sale.

"Hello, Trish," Debbie said.

"Hello, Debbieeee... sweetieeee, how are you?" said Trish. "Will you and your friend sit with me for a minute?"

"We'd love to. I'm fine. How are you?" Trish didn't answer.

They sat down at one of the tables, and a waitress came to take Trish's order. She ordered cheese and bread.

"How are you, Trish?" Debbie asked her again.

"I'm doing fine. But have you heard anything about Cindy?" Trish asked as she darted her eyes around.

"Cindy? You mean the one who works at the lab?" Debbie tilted her head to the side.

"Yes, that's the one. She's missing. I thought you might know something." Trish said. Her hands were fidgety.

"No, I don't. I haven't heard anything about her." Debbie leaned forward.

"I had been calling her for a while, and she wasn't answering her phone. You know, Cindy and I are friends." Her eyes didn't seem to blink enough.

"No, I didn't know." Debbie gazed at Trish with sudden focus. Patty continued to say nothing.

"So, anyway, I went to her house, and she wasn't there. Her whole house was empty, and all her belongings vanished." Trish's eyes looked bloodshot.

Cindy was someone that Debbie had known many years before when she was a technician at the lab. That was where Debbie had met Ed, and come to think of it, that was where Debbie had met Judy too. *That's an interesting coincidence.* Judy wasn't answering her phone either.

"Cindy just completely vanished." Trish continued.

"Maybe she moved?" Debbie offered.

"No, that couldn't be. If Cindy had been moving, she would have told me. I'm one of her best friends. She would never do that." Trish kept looking over her shoulder.

"I'm sorry to hear about your friend. By the way, would you like to buy a crate of wine? We have a discount." Debbie asked. *Apparently, I have no shame.*

Trish's fingers touched her parting lips. "I guess so." She answered.

***

When Debbie got home that night, she watched her favorite program, Crime Investigation, and spent more time with Fluffy. But she couldn't take her mind off her friends, Cindy and Judy. The fact that Cindy had suddenly disappeared, along with all her belongings, was certainly a mystery. She decided to check her Facebook page to see if she could find any clues. She turned on her laptop and went to Facebook, where she saw Cindy's profile. Everything seemed to be expected. Debbie looked at her phone to see if she had received any new messages. *Judy is usually better at getting back to me than this. She reasoned that it might be worth it to look at Judy's Facebook page too.*

Debbie typed in Judy's name and clicked on her profile. *Everything seems to be in order. That's Judy, alright.* The picture was of an older brunette woman with bangs and black-rimmed glasses. Then she went to Judy's husband, Dan's, Facebook profile. Judy, like Cindy, was a technician, but Dan, like Ed, was a nuclear scientist.

He also worked in the lab. She went to his Facebook profile to see that he had posted something recently. She saw the picture of the gray-haired man with a frown on his face. His hair was short, and he had a burgundy sweater on. His post read:

Hello world, or maybe I should say goodbye. I had a great run. It's been enjoyable. Just remember that everything I do has a purpose. Judy, my wonderful wife, I love you. Goodbye to everyone so friendly to me.

Is this a suicide note? What the hell? What could he possibly be saying?

Debbie was perplexed as to why he was saying goodbye to everyone, including his wife. *Are they splitting up?* Debbie had no idea what was happening since there were so many parts to this puzzle. Their house wasn't that far away from hers. She made a mental note to go over there in the morning and check whether they were alright. She wondered whether he had killed himself or if it was all in her head.

Perhaps she wasn't thinking clearly. She had consumed an entire bottle of wine again.

***

Debbie went to Judy and Dan's place before work in the morning. It was a two-story blue house with white rims and pillars. There was no response when she rang the doorbell. She walked up to the window and gazed in. It looked like it was completely empty. *Strange.* That's precisely what Trish said about Cindy's home. *It makes no sense.* She remembered that Judy used to keep a key concealed in a porcelain frog statue. The statue was still there.

Debbie looked inside the frog. There was, in fact, a key in it. She opened the door and walked inside. It was completely empty. There was absolutely nothing in it.

***

Ed paced around his motel room on the fake wood floor. He stared at the orange wall in front of him. He decided to stay at the Motel Six to save money. After all, he'd already withdrawn $15,000 from his account. He had to do what he could to be frugal. He packed all the money into a suitcase. He sent a text: Where *should I drop off the money?* He got a text back: *leave it on the sidewalk of Enrique's Taco Shop. We'll pick it up.* That seemed like an odd request.

He typed: *How will I know that you're picking it up and not someone else?* After all, he wanted the transaction to go smoothly. He was hoping that it would be over fast, and he would never have to deal with these people again.

A text came in: *You'll know it's us because I'll give you a thumbs-up signal.* Ed looked at his watch. It was almost time. *How did I get myself into this situation?* This was something he had never expected to happen. He never imagined his life would turn out like this.

He drove to the taco shop and dropped off the suitcase where he'd been directed. Timidly, he got into his car, rolled down his window, and waited. A man in a suit, wearing sunglasses, went by and plucked the luggage from the ground. He looked at Ed and gave him a thumbs up. The transaction was completed successfully.

Ed hoped that that would be the last of it. He returned to his motel. He was ready to go on with his life at this point. He hoped that everything would return to normal now.

***

Debbie was still not ready to talk about Ed yet. But it seemed that was all Patty wanted to talk about. She did want to tell Patty about Judy's disappearance, although she still wasn't entirely sure that Judy had disappeared. She may have moved. Debbie wasn't sure it was a good idea to talk to anyone about it yet.

"Haven't we discussed the Ed issue a million times? Why do we need to keep talking about it?"

"I understand that you don't want to talk about it. I know that you're living in denial, but I think there is something more we should discuss. I believe you should attend your mother's dinner."

"Wow, it is true that news travels fast. How did you know about that?" Debbie pinched her lips together.

"She invited me and told me to try to talk you into going," Patty said to her in a steady lower-pitched voice.

"Of course, she did. I should have guessed. Aren't you aware that my mother is the devil in a dress?" Debbie blinked rapidly.

"She's going to make my favorite pie, which I haven't eaten in a long time. And there are going to be men there. Do you know how long it has been since I've been to a dinner where there are men? I don't have much of a life. The only thing I ever do is work. And, since Charles left, I haven't met anybody new. It could benefit you to make new acquaintances and meet new people." Patty leaned in.

"Ed and I have only been separated for two days, and already everyone seems to think I should meet someone new." Debbie stumped over her own words.

"Please?" Patty gazed at Debbie alertly.

"OK, fine, let's go." Debbie inhaled deeply. *Here we go.*

***

Debbie didn't want to go to the party, but she felt she had no choice. Her mom was persuading her to go, and Patty was in on it too. She had said that it was her one and only chance to meet men. *Is Patty living vicariously through me?* Debbie was a good friend and understood that Patty's life was dreary, and she had to do something to make her happy.

Debbie put on a lovely black dress sleeveless dress with a neckline that emphasized her shoulders. The thigh-high slit and "demi-lune" cutouts in the back gave it a seductive touch. She pulled her hair back into an updo and applied red lipstick, which was unusual for her. She usually wore light peach lip gloss.

Patty and Debbie showed up at the party at the same time. They stood and gazed at the home for a few minutes before entering. It was a large home, the type that most American children fantasized about growing up in. It featured turrets, gables, dormers, balconies, a screened-in front porch, a free-standing garage, a gazebo, a pool, and formal gardens. It was the American dream, and it was tucked away amid trees.

"You grew up here?" Patty asked.

"It was hell." Debbie insisted.

"I wish I had grown up in your hell," Patty stated.

They walked in together. Once inside, they saw a giant curving staircase that looked like it very likely led to heaven and a lobby large enough to contain the Serengeti. Polished oak flooring and a beautiful banister led to a lofty second-floor gallery. The floor was adorned with a Persian rug. Debbie's mother approached them.

"You're late, Deborah. You're always late." Debbie's mom was blinking rapidly.

The maid came to take their coats.

"It's OK," Debbie said. "I can put my coat in the closet myself." Debbie lifted her chin into the air sharply.

"Deborah, let her do it. It's her job." Debbie's mom said to her, breaking eye contact.

"OK." Debbie handed her coat over.

"You look particularly nice tonight. What happened? You usually look so masculine and casual. I love those heels." Debbie's mom pinched her lips together.

"Oh, these heels? Really? Because I feel like I'm going to fall over and sprain my ankle, which doesn't seem like it would be very feminine." Debbie smirked as she said it.

"You're not going to fall over, Deborah; you're always so dramatic." *Me? Dramatic? Mom is the one who is over the top. She talks like she is from New England, which she isn't.*

Debbie's mom saw a man walk by. She called out to him. "Craig! Can you come over here?"

"Yes, of course." The man obliged and came their way.

"This is Craig. He's a researcher. Well, I'll have to leave you all to get acquainted. I have some things to attend to." *Things to attend to? This is your house? What could you have to attend to?* Debbie's mom left them with Craig. He was a softly fat, balding, incredibly chirpy, wholly colorless, ridiculously boyish-looking man.

"Craig, I'm Deborah, I mean, Debbie. And this is Patty." Debbie said as she breathed in deeply.

Craig looked at Patty and said with an upturned face. "Has anyone ever told you that the color of your eyes is like squirrels' fur?"

"No, I don't think so. No one has told me that, not yet." Patty raised her eyebrows.

"Well, they are. And that's a compliment." Craig smiled.

"Thank you very much." Patty looked at him with a questioning gaze.

Debbie asked Craig what he did for a living.

"I work in a think tank. I do statistical analysis. I can't give specifics." He answered, speaking rapidly.

"Statistics?" Patty asked. She looked confused.

"That's a type of math," Debbie whispered to her. Patty looked disappointed.

She whispered to Debbie, "I don't like math."

"That sounds like an interesting job. What kinds of things are you studying?" Debbie's jaw was visibly tight.

"I can't tell you." *Oh no, that sounds just like Ed's job. Not the kind of person I want to be around.*

"I can't tell you the details about my job, but I could tell you some fun statistics." Craig appeared very relaxed.

"Fun statistics?" Debbie asked. "I didn't know there were such things."

"Oh, yes, statistics can be entertaining. Did you know that the average person eats almost 1500 pounds of food a year?" Craig's movements were fluid.

"No, I didn't. That's a fun fact." Debbie said sarcastically.

"Did you know that the human eye blinks an average of 4,200,000 times a year?" His eyes danced and sparkled.

"I didn't know that either." *I don't think I really wanted to know that.* "Maybe I should try to count my blinks. By the way, don't you think we should get away from the doorway and move to where the drinks are being served?" Debbie asked.

"Indeed," Craig said. The others followed Debbie to the cart in the other living room, where wine was served. It had oversized wall art, giving it a chic and high-impact design, something that would make heads turn and start conversations. Debbie remembered when her mom was designing that room. She had explained the whole thing to Debbie. *Maybe that's where everything went wrong.*

Debbie filled her glass to the brim with wine, hoping it would help her get through the night, and then sat on the couch. The other two followed her lead, sitting down next to her.

"No, no, don't try to count. That would be impossible." Craig said.

"Count what?" Debbie asked.

"Your blinks," Craig said politely.

"Oh, I had forgotten," Debbie replied, smirking.

"Maybe after the party, I could read to you both for an hour or two from my book Fun Statistical Facts. I've memorized information from it so I can use it at parties and engage in good conversations." His voice was light and bubbly. *Where is mom right now? What things is she attending to?*

"That's very nice," Debbie replied. *Boring, boring, boring.* Debbie's mom walked in and announced that dinner was served.

It was finally time for dinner to begin. *Thank God. I could eat a horse.* They sat at the table together in the dining room. The dining room had a subtle glamour about it with a penchant for comfort. Debbie remembered when her mother told her that dining room tables are subtle statement-makers and that the combination creates a luxury eating space when lighting is well-chosen. *A luxury eating space? This house really was the source of my dysfunction. My mom was great at creating luxury eating spaces but terrible at understanding me or making me feel like she cared.*

Craig was in the middle, and Patty and Debbie were on either side of him. They were served bibb lettuce salad, brie on grilled bread, and sesame chicken in acorn squash.

Craig turned to Patty. "Patty, do you cook?" he asked, sitting straight up.

"Yes." Patty wiggled in her chair.

"Are you a good housekeeper?" He tapped his fingers on the table lightly.

"Yes. Pretty good." Patty's posture became stiff.

"How do you feel about the institution of marriage?" Craig took a bite, seeming to savor his food.

"The what? Oh... I'm not opposed to it." She covered her mouth.

The night seemed to go on and on. Debbie was thankful when the apple pie finally came after the meal. Her mother had said very little, except "that's very interesting" to all of Craig's fun facts. Patty excused herself early. Debbie didn't blame her. She needed to remove herself too. She couldn't handle any more of Craig's fun facts.

Debbie came up with an excuse, saying she had things to attend to and left. Then she realized that Craig had followed her out.

"I had a wonderful time tonight." He said. "Can you give my number to your friend, Patty? She's gorgeous. I was hoping that she would go out with me sometime."

"Unfortunately, I'm pretty sure she is seeing someone." Debbie lied.

"Oh, that's too bad. I liked her. She cooks. She does housework. She's comfortable with the institution of marriage. I'm getting old, and I need a wife. Believe it or not, I've asked many women to marry me, but none have accepted."

"Oh, I see, that's surprising," Debbie said to be polite.

"I don't suppose you would want to see me again...."

***

After coming home from the terrible party, Debbie changed into something more comfortable. She watched her favorite show again with Fluffy. She thought about what Trish had said earlier about Cindy. She thought about how strange it was to see Judy's empty house. She thought about how strange it was that Trish still had not returned her call, which was not like her. She thought about Dan's bazaar Facebook post. *Did Judy and Dan move, or was something more sinister?*

What are the chances that Cindy and Judy darted without telling anyone where they were going? That doesn't seem like Judy. She'd been a long-time resident of that neighborhood. *Why would she do such a thing without informing anyone? Where could they possibly be? Why am I not doing anything? I should go check on Judy to see if she's OK.* Perhaps, since she wasn't in her home, she was in her cabin. Debbie hoped that there was some reasonable explanation for what was going on.

***

She drove to the cabin later that evening to check whether Judy was there. It was quite a distance away. To get there, she'd have to travel for an hour. Although it wasn't something she wanted to do, she needed answers to figure out what was going on with Judy and Dan. That night, as she traveled up the

36

mountain. She drove past dark tree trunks and shadows and almost hit overhanging limbs that were strewn across the road seen at the last second.

She nearly drove off the road a couple of times since it was a little slippery. On the side of the road were clumps of bushes, barely visible black trails snaking through the undergrowth, and the moon was shining through a lattice of leaves. She could see patchy sky and stars in glimpses through tree breaks. Tall shadowed pines stretched up like arrows into the atmosphere.

When she arrived at the cabin, she saw no vehicles parked in the driveway. *What could be going on?* She went to the door and rang the doorbell. The house was beautiful. She certainly would have enjoyed staying there. The oversized porch looked inviting. It would have been a nice place to sit, relax, and take in the view on the porch swing or one of the lounge chairs. She glanced through the window, but all the blinds were pulled down, and she couldn't see anything.

She looked at the door and noticed that it was open slightly. The doorknob looked like it had been damaged, and the lock appeared broken. She opened the door and walked in. There was nothing unusual about what she saw. It seemed to be a typical cabin. There were some excellent sofas in the living area and a fireplace. It was also spotless. She was met with a large vaulted ceiling, hickory hardwood floors, and a plethora of furniture that appeared handmade. It would be a great place to watch a movie, start the gas log fireplace, and cuddle up on the couch with someone special. It would have been fun to have stayed there with Ed back when things were good.

It suddenly occurred to Debbie, *what if Judy thinks I'm an intruder?*

"Judy?" she began to call out to her. "It's me, Debbie." She didn't want Judy to mistake her for an intruder and shoot her.

There was no response. There seemed to be no one there. "Judy, are you alright?"

Debbie went toward the bedroom of the cabin. The door to the bedroom was ajar. Debbie opened the door and walked in, only to see Judy lying on the floor. Debbie immediately froze and listened to see if it sounded like anyone else was nearby. "Oh my God, Judy!" She checked her pulse. Judy was dead.

Seriously, what the fuck is going on? Who would have killed Judy? She was the sweetest woman in the world. It was evident that she hadn't taken her own life. The wound was in her back. Just then, she heard a disturbance outside the bushes at that exact moment. *Oh my god, the murderer is still here.*

Debbie flew to the corner of the room and crouched down, hiding so no one would see her from the window. She realized the window was open because she could feel a draft coming in.

"Debbie," she heard a man's voice say from outside the window.

Oh, my God, he knows my name.

Then she realized she had recognized the voice. "Ed?" She got up and looked out the window. "Why are you here?" Ed was standing outside the window.

"I wanted to know if Judy was OK," Ed said defensively.

"You're wondering if Judy is OK? You barely know who she is." Debbie answered, feeling confused.

"We worked in the lab together. I knew her there." Ed said like it was apparent.

"But she was *my* friend," Debbie answered in a possessive tone. Why are you hiding in the bushes."

Ed looked at Debbie, but no words would come.

"Ed, can you meet me in the front, so we don't have to talk through a window?" Debbie insisted.

She walked to the front of the cabin, but Ed was nowhere to be found.

Where is Ed? Did he run away from the scene of the crime?

***

Debbie called the police to report the murder. They asked her a few questions, and she went home. She was utterly exhausted from the ordeal and slept in the following day. In the morning, she got up and poured herself a cup of coffee, feeling groggy and out of sorts. *Thank God it's Saturday. I couldn't go to work with all this on my mind. It's been one helluva week!*

She sat in her dining room, sipping her coffee, when she heard the doorbell ring. *Who could it be?* She thought. *If it's Ed, he has some explaining to do.*

It was a man dressed in a police uniform. He was tall, dark, and handsome and had a smile that could melt any woman's heart. *Oh my God, look at those teeth. He's beautiful.*

"Can I come in and ask you some questions?" He asked.

"The police already questioned me last night." She replied.

"I understand that ma'am, but I'm a detective. I'm with a different division. It's customary for the head detective to question all witnesses thoroughly." He insisted.

"OK, come on in," Debbie said.

"Would you like some coffee."

"No, thank you."

He unclipped his bag and sat down. He put it on his lap. Debbie also sat down. He pulled 2 passports out of his bag.

The police officer handed Debbie a passport. "Do you know anything about this?"

Debbie looked at it. It had a picture of Judy but with a different name, Agatha Meier. It said she was a citizen of Switzerland. "I didn't know Judy was Swiss."

"How about this one?" He handed her another passport. This one said that Judy was a citizen of China. Her name was written in Chinese script, or so Debbie assumed. *Judy is Chinese and Swiss?* It didn't make any sense. She didn't look Chinese.

"No, I don't know about this," Debbie answered, fumbling her words.

"How about this one?" He handed her a third passport. This one said she was a citizen of North Korea. *There is no way that she is North Korean. What is going on?*

She grimaced and frowned. "I don't know why she would have this either."

"Where were you on the night of the murder?" The officer asked.

"When did the murder take place?" Debbie rubbed her chin.

"At 9 o'clock PM yesterday." He offered.

"Oh, I was with my dog, Fluffy." She was blinking rapidly now.

"What were you doing?" The officer touched the base of his neck.

"We were talking, hanging out, watching TV. And I was drinking some wine." Debbie started swallowing excessively.

That's very interesting. "So, Fluffy, your dog, when you talk to him, does he talk back?" *What kind of question is that?* The police officer had a serious look on his face.

"No, he doesn't talk back to me." Her body posture collapsed a little.

"So, if we were to question your dog concerning your alibi, would he confirm your story?" The officer asked as he tugged on his ear.

She bit her lip. "No, he's a dog." The police officer wrote down some notes about that.

Was he just teasing me, or did he think I was crazy?

"I'm just teasing you, Ma'am. By the way, do you like Chinese? I'm hungry."